From Tadpole to Frog

By STEVEN ANDERSON

Illustrated by MARCIN PIWOWARSKI

CANTATA
LEARNING

MANKATO, MINNESOTA

WWW.CANTATALEARNING.COM

CANTATA LEARNING

MANKATO, MINNESOTA

Published by Cantata Learning
1710 Roe Crest Drive
North Mankato, MN 56003
www.cantatalearning.com

Library of Congress Control Number: 2014956999
978-1-63290-263-4 (hardcover/CD)
978-1-63290-415-7 (paperback/CD)
978-1-63290-457-7 (paperback)

From Tadpole to Frog by Steven Anderson
Illustrated by Marcin Piwowarski

Book design, Tim Palin Creative
Editorial direction, Flat Sole Studio
Executive musical production and direction, Elizabeth Draper
Music arranged and produced by Steven C Music

Printed in the United States of America.

VISIT

WWW.CANTATALEARNING.COM/ACCESS-OUR-MUSIC

TO SING ALONG TO THE SONG

Every animal changes during its life.
A frog starts as a tiny egg. A tadpole
hatches from the egg. As it **matures**, the
tadpole loses its tail and grows legs.
Then it becomes an adult frog and
mates so new eggs can hatch. This
series of changes is called a **life cycle**.

Now turn the page,
and sing along.

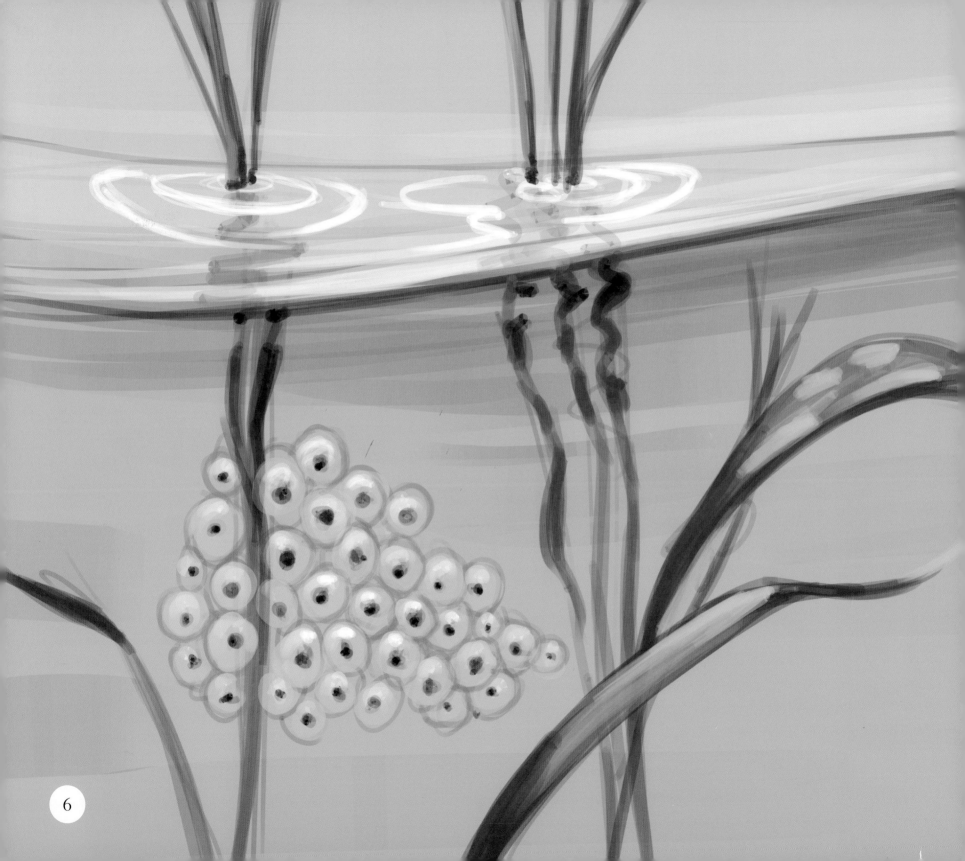

A frog doesn't have just one egg at a time.

She can lay hundreds, all covered in slime.

Out pops a tadpole, with **gills** and a tail.

It swims around with the fish and the snails.

There's a cycle of life
for all living things.

Frogs begin as tadpoles
and then start growing
up, up, up into adults.

The cycle's never ending.

When the tadpole begins to sprout tiny legs,
it's ready to hop into life's next stage.

It becomes a froglet after growing lungs,
and then it's able to breathe in **oxygen**!

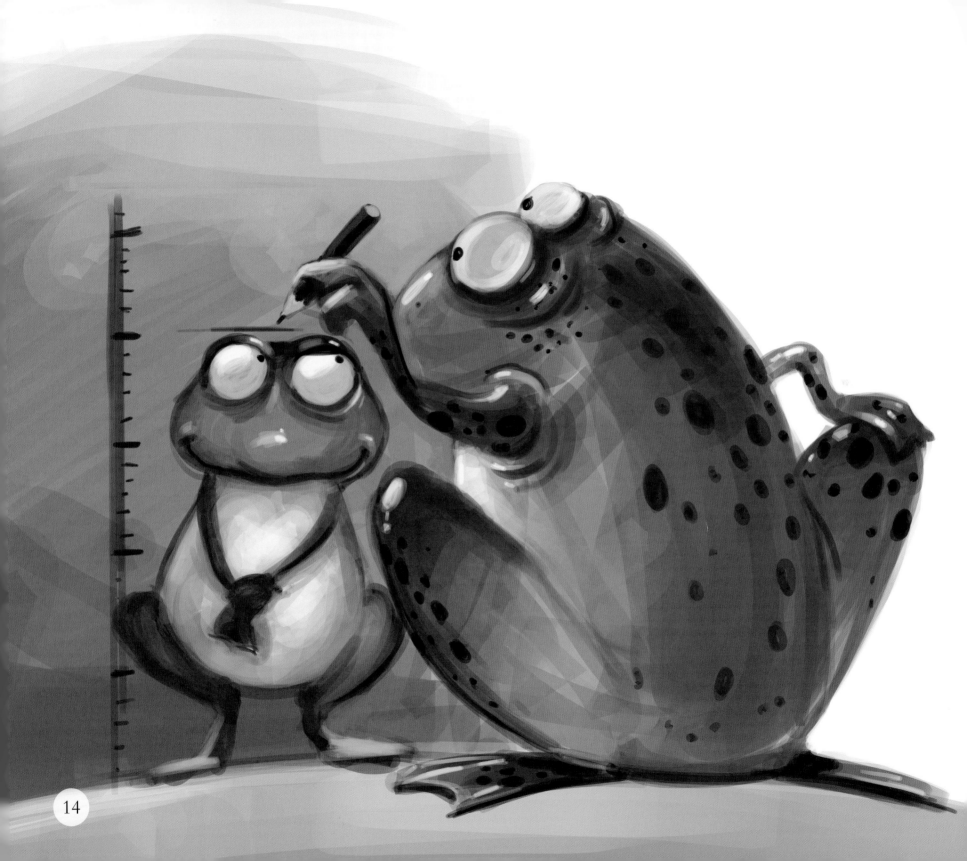

There's a cycle of life
for all living things.

Frogs begin as tadpoles
and then start growing
up, up, up into adults.

The cycle's never ending.

The frog starts to hop around on lily pads
and loses the tail that it once had.

Then as an adult, the frog looks for a match.

One day, more eggs will be ready to hatch.

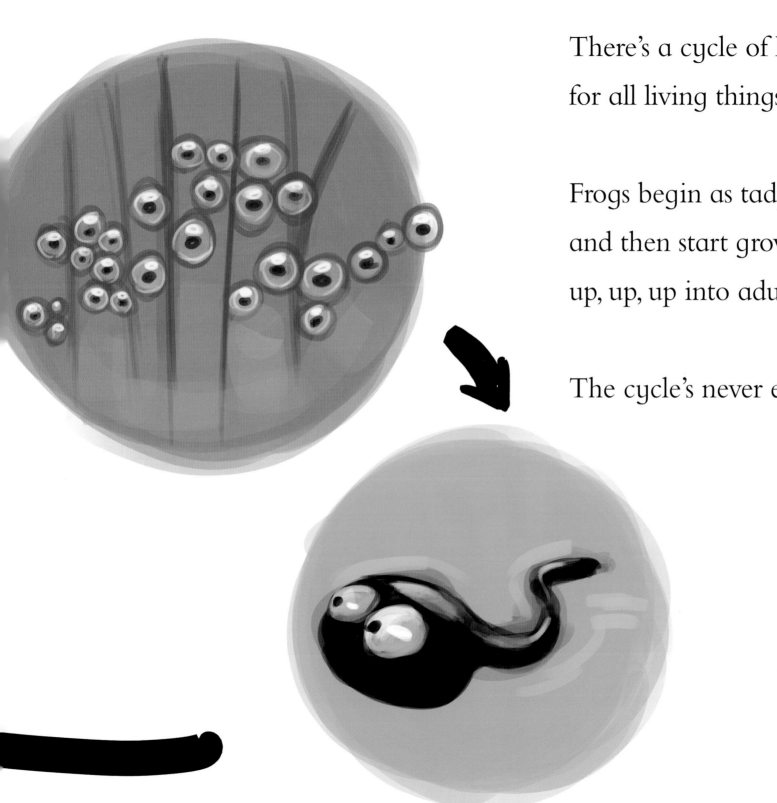

There's a cycle of life
for all living things.

Frogs begin as tadpoles
and then start growing
up, up, up into adults.

The cycle's never ending.

SONG LYRICS
From Tadpole to Frog

A frog doesn't have just one egg at a time.
She can lay hundreds, all covered in slime.

Out pops a tadpole, with gills and a tail.
It swims around with the fish and the snails.

There's a cycle of life
for all living things.

Frogs begin as tadpoles
and then start growing
up, up, up into adults.

The cycle's never ending.

When the tadpole begins to sprout
    tiny legs,
it's ready to hop into life's next stage.

It becomes a froglet after growing lungs,
and then it's able to breathe in oxygen!

There's a cycle of life
for all living things.

Frogs begin as tadpoles
and then start growing
up, up, up into adults.

The cycle's never ending.

The frog starts to hop around on lily pads
and loses the tail that it once had.

Then as an adult, the frog looks for a
    match.
One day, more eggs will be ready to hatch.

There's a cycle of life
for all living things.

Frogs begin as tadpoles
and then start growing
up, up, up into adults.

The cycle's never ending.

From Tadpole to Frog

Pop
Steven C Music

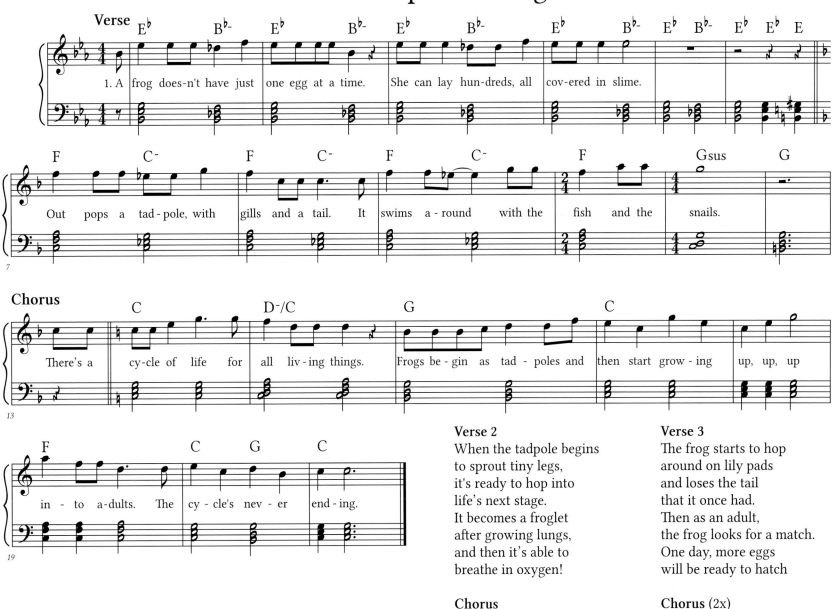

Verse 2
When the tadpole begins
to sprout tiny legs,
it's ready to hop into
life's next stage.
It becomes a froglet
after growing lungs,
and then it's able to
breathe in oxygen!

Chorus

Verse 3
The frog starts to hop
around on lily pads
and loses the tail
that it once had.
Then as an adult,
the frog looks for a match.
One day, more eggs
will be ready to hatch

Chorus (2x)

GLOSSARY

gills—organs that tadpoles and fish use to get oxygen out of the water

life cycle—a series of changes an animal goes through, from birth to growing into an adult

mates—to pair up and produce young

matures—grows into an adult

oxygen—a colorless gas found in air and water; all animals need oxygen to survive.

GUIDED READING ACTIVITIES

1. Who is the illustrator of this book? What is your favorite illustration and why?

2. List the stages of a frog's life cycle. How are they all different from each other?

3. What is another possible title for this book?

TO LEARN MORE

Appleby, Alex. *I See a Frog*. New York: Gareth Stevens Pub., 2013.

Ganeri, Anita. *Frogs and Tadpoles*. Mankato, MN: Amicus, 2011.

Guillain, Charlotte. *Life Story of a Frog*. Chicago: Heinemann Library, 2015.

Sweeney, Alyse. *Frogs*. Mankato, MN: Capstone Press, 2010.